Getting Through Grief

FOR YOUTH

Eight Biblical Gifts
for Living with Loss

MICHAEL W. NEWMAN

CONCORDIA PUBLISHING HOUSE · SAINT LOUIS

For Harley and Layne

You'll need this one day. We all do.

Published by Concordia Publishing House
3558 S. Jefferson Ave., St. Louis, MO 63118-3968
1-800-325-3040 • cph.org

Manufactured in the United States of America

1 2 3 4 5 6 7 8 9 10 30 29 28 27 26 25 24 23 22 21

CONTENTS

THE SEVENTH GIFT: **PURPOSE**

THE EIGHTH GIFT: **PRESENCE**

Out of the Pit

Dear friend, at this moment, you may be feeling really sad or hurt or heartbroken. Loss feels terrible—it *is* terrible, but please know there is hope.

Your loss and pain do not have the last word.

Sometimes, grief makes you feel like you've been thrown into a deep, dark pit with no way out. But before you give up and surrender to the darkness, I have good news for you: there is a way out. Joy is possible. **You will make it through this.**

Guess what? **Your sadness, weakness, and pain are where God meets you.** You may not feel it or even believe it, but in your darkness, God draws near to give you gifts that release you from gloom, restore your soul, and bless you with strength for each day.

You can't get out of grief's pit under your own power, but God will lift you out.

King David experienced heartbreak and loss. He said, "*I waited patiently for the Lord; He inclined to me and heard my cry. He drew me up from the pit of destruction, out of the miry bog, and set my feet upon a rock, making my steps secure*" (Psalm 40:1–2).

God's specialty is lifting people out of the pit. How? Not by bending over and reaching in but by getting into the pit with people and lifting them out. That's why He sent Jesus. Jesus came to be with you in your sadness. On the cross, Jesus carried your heartbreak. And when Jesus rose from the dead, He broke suffering's hold on you.

The dark pit doesn't win. Jesus does—and because of Him, so do you.

This book shares **eight gifts** to carry you through your journey of grief. These gifts will help you. They will provide relief from the pit of sadness. They will help you get through your hurt.

Are you ready to receive help in your heartbreak? Jesus is with you. He will carry you through.

Getting Through It

WORD: How does Psalm 40:1–2 give you hope in your heartbreak?

WRESTLE: Ask God to help you with what your heart needs most right now.

WATCH: Talk to an adult you trust about why you're sad. How does the advice you hear help you?

Speaking Up

The first gift God gives is conversation. He starts the conversation. You get to respond.

God's part of the conversation is His Word, the Bible. That's where He speaks to you. Your part of the conversation is prayer. That's how you get to speak to Him.

This powerful conversation is a gift that will start breaking down sadness and hopelessness. It will be a lifeline that strengthens you.

What does God say in His Word?

First, He tells you the truth about life: your life is not perfect, and sometimes, terrible things happen.

Second, He tells you the truth about Himself: He is sad about your tears and pain—He cares about you. He is with you.

God will heal your heart, and He will bring you through it.

God's promises are true. His action is a fact. **The proof is in Jesus.** He is real. He came to help you and to save you. He wants to hear from you.

That's why God invites you: *"Call upon Me in the day of trouble; I will deliver you, and you shall glorify Me"* (Psalm 50:15).

God speaks; you pray. I'm not just talking about a prayer before you eat or at bedtime. **I'm talking about replacing your inner voices of doubt and sadness with prayer.**

You know how your mind wants to tell you that all is lost, that no one cares, that you'll never feel better, and that this hurt and anger will never change. Those voices are *not* true.

Instead of letting those voices rule your life and fill your mind, God lets you lift your voice to Him. Your prayers turn hurt into hope.

Go ahead and ask God questions. Ask Him the tough questions. Tell Him about your pain. Ask for help. Say thank You for blessings. God listens to you. **He promises never to leave you or forsake you.**

Keep listening. Keep praying. The pit will lose its power.

Getting Through It

WORD: What does God promise you in Psalm 50:15?

WRESTLE: Say a prayer right now, telling God about your trouble and asking Him for His help.

WATCH: Find a Bible reading plan that will keep God's voice in your life every day.

How to Pray

You don't have to be "good" at prayer to pray. Sometimes, prayer is messy and awkward. Sometimes, your words are more like shouts or groans.

When the Bible invites you to cast "all your anxieties" on God (1 Peter 5:7), it paints a picture of throwing your troubles at God.

Sometimes, your prayers are more like wordless groans from deep inside your heart and soul. The Bible even says: *"Likewise the Spirit helps us in our weakness. For we do not know what to pray for as we ought, but the Spirit Himself intercedes for us with groanings too deep for words"* (Romans 8:26).

How do you pray? Ask God your questions. Groan your groans. Call upon God in the day of trouble (Psalm 50:15). Cast your burdens upon Him (Psalm 55:22). Confess your failures and ask Him for mercy (Psalm 51). Thank Him for His goodness (Psalms 107; 136). Ask Him for help (Psalm 70). Wrestle with Him as you hurt (Psalm 27).

Keep crying out to God. Keep listening to God's Word. That's the key to prayer.

One evening, a worried and stressed-out Jacob wrestled with God (Genesis 32:22–31). All night, Jacob refused to let go. When morning came, even after he had suffered an injury to his hip, Jacob said to God, *"I will not let You go unless You bless me"* (v. 26). And God did bless Jacob with a new name and a new future as he limped into the new day.

God speaks to you in His Word. Now you are invited to wrestle with Him in prayer. Don't worry about how pretty your prayer sounds. Talk to God. Plead and cry; groan and ask. **But don't let go—no matter how long it takes—until you receive His blessing and help.**

Your Savior is faithful. You may be limping, but Jesus will carry you into a new hope and future.

Getting Through It

WORD: Which psalm can you relate to most from the ones mentioned in this devotion?

WRESTLE: Tell God something about your sadness that you can't understand. Ask Him to lead you through it.

WATCH: Look for one way God is helping or strengthening you today. Write it here.

Becoming a Listener

I will be honest with you: my life growing up was not easy or happy. By the time my parents finally divorced, a lot of damage had been done. You may understand what it feels like to be in a broken family or relationship.

How did I get through it? What was my lifeline? **The gift of prayer.**

I talked, I asked questions, I shared ideas, I gave thanks, and I tearfully called out to God for help.

Prayer kept me going. But it became even more to me. **It turned into a lion tamer's whip that stopped roars of hopelessness, shame, sadness, worry, depression, and self-destruction.**

**If you want to get through heartbreak,
listen to God and pray to God.**

The apostle Paul wrote, "*Do not be anxious about anything, but in everything by prayer and supplication with thanksgiving let your requests be made known to God. And the peace of God, which surpasses all understanding, will guard your hearts and your minds in Christ Jesus*" (Philippians 4:6–7).

In *everything*, lift up your prayers.

What might it look like if you made your whole life and every thought a conversation with God? When you're doubting, sad, angry, or confused, what if you made it all a prayer? Instead of worrying or getting angry, what if you said a prayer?

**The gift of conversation—God's Word and prayer—
will free you from the dark pit of sadness and pain.**

Remember, prayer is a gift to share. If you understand grief, you will be able to listen to people and pray for them. You can share Jesus' help by showing the love and care you receive from Him.

Getting Through It

WORD: What is peace that "surpasses all understanding"?

WRESTLE: Make a prayer plan today. When will you read God's Word, and how will you replace worry or anxiety with regular prayer?

WATCH: Find someone who needs a good listener. Listen to their troubles and pray for them.

Anger

When I was in third grade, two thieves walked into my grandfather's dry cleaner's in Chicago. They wanted money, but when Grandpa didn't open the cash drawer fast enough, one of the robbers shot him in the chest. Not long after that, he died. My family and I were crushed.

If you've been through any kind of violent loss, you understand all the feelings that fill your heart. One huge feeling I had during that time was anger. How could someone do this? I hated that man and felt he deserved to die.

When you're hurt, you have every right to be angry, but be careful! **Anger has a way of taking over your life and turning you into a bitter and miserable person.**

That's why God gives a second gift to lift you out of the pit: forgiveness. In the New Testament, to forgive means "to release" or "to let go."

You may not be able to solve or fix your hurt, but God invites you to hand it over to Him.

People who hurt you may never say they're sorry. But God lets you give your pain to Him. Psalm 4:4–5 says, *"Be angry, and do not sin; ponder in your own hearts on your beds, and be silent. Offer right sacrifices, and put your trust in the Lord."* Anger is an important and real emotion, but letting anger take control of your life will destroy you and others. Instead of holding on to anger, God calls you to give it away—to give it to Him. **That is where forgiveness begins.**

The gift of forgiveness will release you from your pit of pain because it's on the shoulders of the One who can handle it.

You don't have to hold on to your hurt. Keep giving it to God.

Getting Through It

WORD: What new way does Psalm 4:4 give you to handle your feelings?

WRESTLE: What feelings do you need to let go of and give to God today?

WATCH: Ask God to carry the pain you're feeling so you can be free.

Regret

When I speak with people who have experienced loss, I notice that, sometimes, they feel guilty.

If you're sad and grieving, you may be feeling guilty because you messed up in some way. You may have hurt someone's feelings. You may be thinking hateful thoughts.

You may hear people say, "Don't worry about it," but guilt and regret can steal joy and hope from you.

This is where the second gift comes in: **you need the life-rescuing and guilt-erasing gift of forgiveness.**

Forgiveness doesn't mean saying, "It's okay" or "Don't worry about it." Forgiveness actually removes guilt and puts sin to death.

One of the Old Testament words for forgiveness means "to carry" and "to take away." In ancient times, when people sinned, the guilty person brought a goat or a lamb to the priest. The priest placed his hand on the head of the animal and killed it as a sin offering. The animal "carried" the guilt as a substitute for the guilty person. The sin would literally be put to death and carried away. This sacrifice ritual happened every year.

Ancient religious sacrifices used animals. **But there was one sacrifice that brought complete and lasting forgiveness. It was the one-time sacrifice of Jesus, God's own Son.**

God's Word explains: "[*Jesus*] *has no need, like those high priests, to offer sacrifices daily, first for His own sins and then for those of the people, since He did this once for all when He offered up Himself*" (Hebrews 7:27).

Forgiveness "once for all" came through Jesus. He carried your guilt. He took your sin. All of it was put to death when He breathed His last breath on the cross. The impossible was done.

Through Jesus, you are blessed with the gift that releases you from the pit of guilt and shame. You have been forgiven.

Getting Through It

WORD: What did Jesus' sacrifice on the cross accomplish for you?

WRESTLE: What are you feeling guilty about?

WATCH: In prayer, ask for God's forgiveness. If there's someone you need to say you're sorry to, tell them this week.

The Past

What about your past? Do you feel like you've missed out because of your loss? Do you feel like your life will never be normal because of your hurt? How can you live in freedom from grief?

Let's take a closer look at the gift of God's forgiveness.

Jesus' life, death, and resurrection free you from being held captive by the past. Isaiah 53:5 says this about Jesus: *"But He was pierced for our transgressions . . . and with His wounds we are healed."* Jesus heals you and sets you free from your hurt. But there's more.

God not only releases you from your past—He *changes* your past.

God rewrites your history with His grace.

That's why God's Word says: *"Do you not know that all of us who have been baptized into Christ Jesus were baptized into His death? We were buried therefore with Him by baptism into death, in order that, just as Christ was raised from the dead by the glory of the Father,* ***we too might walk in newness of life****"* (Romans 6:3–4, emphasis added). Your old life was taken away by Jesus and your new life was raised up when Baptism washed your sins away.

Your past is gone: *"Therefore, if anyone is in Christ, he is a new creation. The old has passed away; behold, the new has come"* (2 Corinthians 5:17).

Jesus earned the gift. The Holy Spirit delivered it in Baptism.

God doesn't even remember the old you. He can't recall your failures and faults. Why? It is no longer you who lives, but Christ who lives in you (Galatians 2:20).

The gift of forgiveness gives you a new beginning today. You can trust that God's grace lifts you out of the pit and lets you live a new life.

Getting Through It

WORD: What fact about forgiveness stands out most to you from the Bible verses in this devotion?

WRESTLE: What thought or event from the past keeps bringing hurt to your heart?

WATCH: Ask God to take away the old hurt and to strengthen your faith in the new life He gives you.

Burdens

The gift of forgiveness lifts the burdens that want to crush you. That's good and helpful news. But what is the secret of living new life in that forgiveness instead of letting guilt, wounds, and regrets drag you down?

The secret is to remember who carries your load.

Jesus invites us, *"Come to Me, all who labor and are heavy laden, and I will give you rest"* (Matthew 11:28). Jesus takes your heavy burden and gives you an easy one. Yes, an easy one.

When Jesus does the heavy lifting and handles your struggles, your life is easier.

As a friend of mine used to say, "It's easier to walk with Him than without Him."

Life is easier with Jesus. True, there will still be plenty of trouble. Yes, you'll still experience sadness and stress.

But facing those struggles with Jesus is easier than carrying them yourself.

What does that look like? When an "if only" or a "should have" or a "could have" or a "shouldn't have" begins to drag you into despair or doubt, give it to Jesus immediately. Say, "This is too much for me to figure out or handle, dear Savior. I'm releasing it to You. I can't even think about it." Give it to God in prayer. When someone or something begins to make you feel bad, don't get pulled in. Say, "God, I'm not going there. You need to take care of this."

Practice giving your burdens to Jesus.

Hand them over. Let them go. **Rejoice in the gift of forgiveness that frees you from the pit.** When the old you or a bitter you starts talking, say to God, "That's not me anymore. That's the old me. Ignore that." **Keep piling your troubles on God's shoulders, and you will be lifted up.**

Getting Through It

WORD: How does Matthew 11:28, quoted in this devotion, help you today?

WRESTLE: What thought or feeling tries to drag you into hopelessness?

WATCH: Ask God to take your burden. Write some of the ways He fills you with His peace.

You Are Loved

As you hurt and grieve, you need to know that God has not forgotten about you or left you on your own. He isn't mad at you. He is not ignoring you or punishing you. You may *feel* alone. There are times when God *seems* absent, but it is in those terrible times when you see clearly *why* God chose to be present.

God is your refuge and strength, a very present help *in trouble* (see Psalm 46:1). Not just in case trouble comes. But *in* trouble. Terrible heartbreak and loss happen in this broken world. You and I don't want it that way. We wish hurt, evil, and unfairness did not exist. We want things to be good and to make sense. But too often, they aren't and they don't.

Is this awful situation God's fault? He may be easy to blame, but **God isn't careless or cruel. He came to bring help and hope.**

God revealed Himself *to bring you through* the mess.

That is what Jesus explained in one of the most well-known verses of the Bible. Jesus said, *"For God so loved the world, that He gave His only Son, that whoever believes in Him should not perish but have eternal life"* (John 3:16).

God hasn't given up on you. He isn't ignoring your cries for help. God loves you and is with you. What's the proof? God gave His life for you: *"By this we know love, that [Jesus] laid down His life for us"* (1 John 3:16).

Your pain and grief tell you that you need Jesus.
The good news is this:
He came down to rescue you.

God loves you and will never let you go.

Getting Through It

WORD: What does John 3:16 tell you as you go through your grief? If you haven't memorized this verse, start learning it today.

WRESTLE: Talk to God about how you need the assurance of His love during this difficult time.

WATCH: Note some ways you see God's love as you read God's Word and through the people He puts in your life.

What Love Does

What do you need most when you are hurting? When the worst happens, I want God to take it away, to fix it. I want the reason for the pain to be gone. But what if your loss isn't taken away? What do you need then?

You need strength. You need healing. You need someone to hold on to you. You need help from the outside. You need to be loved by God.

The New Testament word for God's love is *agape*, which means "complete self-sacrifice." That is the kind of love God has for you. **God may not explain everything or fix every problem, but He will carry you through grief.**

God's love will get you through it.

A wise person said to me long ago, "Why don't you just let God love you?" I didn't have to figure everything out. I didn't have to solve the problem. I didn't have to be the person in control. I just needed to *receive* God's love.

Do you need to stop being mad at God and simply receive His love?

His love will build you up (1 Corinthians 8:1). God's love will strengthen you to face life after loss: *"Your steadfast love and Your faithfulness will ever preserve me!"* (Psalm 40:11). God's love will hold you steady: *"When I thought, 'My foot slips,' Your steadfast love, O Lord, held me up"* (Psalm 94:18). When you become stressed and anxious, your faithful God *"will quiet you by His love"* (Zephaniah 3:17). God's love will give you eternal hope because *"His steadfast love endures forever"* (Psalm 136).

God's love is the ultimate and most trustworthy affirmation of your worth.

You can't fight pain with more pain. You don't stop hurt with more hurt. For your dark pit of grief, you need the gift of God's love.

Getting Through It

WORD: God's love is amazing. What verse about God's love in this devotion means the most to you in your sadness?

WRESTLE: Ask God to give you His love that brings you through your loss.

WATCH: Look for a way to show God's agape love to someone in your life.

What Love Looks Like

God's love is your secret weapon of confidence and survival. **As much and as often as possible, place yourself in situations that fill you with God's love.** Read the Bible, be active in your church, listen to Christian music, and have devotions. The apostle Paul prayed that you would *"know the love of Christ that surpasses knowledge, that you may be filled with all the fullness of God"* (Ephesians 3:19).

But watch out! Trouble, pain, and grief will try to get you to go it alone.

Remember, when times are difficult,
you need the strength of your Savior more than ever.

The apostle Paul described God's gift of love in 1 Corinthians 13:

> Love is patient and kind; love does not envy or boast; it is not arrogant or rude. It does not insist on its own way; it is not irritable or resentful; it does not rejoice at wrongdoing, but rejoices with the truth. Love bears all things, believes all things, hopes all things, endures all things. Love never ends. (vv. 4–8)

This description of love applies first to God's love shown to you through Jesus. God is patient with you. He is kind. He meets you where you are. He carries your struggles. He believes in you and has high hopes for you. He accepts you as you are and always forgives. His love for you will never end.

God's love will even surprise you
with good things that come out of bad times.

The Bible promises: *"We know that for those who love God all things work together for good, for those who are called according to His purpose"* (Romans 8:28). God isn't brushing off your pain and telling you not to worry about it. **He is promising that His love will bring blessings even out of your brokenness.** You can count on it.

Getting Through It

WORD: How have you seen God's love as it is described in 1 Corinthians 13:4–8?

WRESTLE: Thank God for blessings—even small ones—that you've seen come out of your difficult times.

WATCH: Pay close attention to people in your life who are showing you God's love. Thank one of them.

Living as One Who Loves

As God's love lifts you out of your pit of sadness, He will give you a new question to ask:

"How can I show God's love to the people in my life today?"

The Bible says, "*We love because* [*God*] *first loved us*" (1 John 4:19). **God's love will pull you out of the dark pit of grief and change the way you live.** As you share God's love with others, you will feel better and will experience even more healing from your pain.

Jesus told a story about the power and impact of God's love. The story was about a young son who hurt his father's feelings in a terrible way. The son walked out, but his plan didn't work. Frightened and ashamed, the son decided to go back home. Jesus revealed what happened:

> While he was still a long way off, his father saw him and felt compassion, and ran and embraced him and kissed him. And the son said to him, "Father, I have sinned against heaven and before you. I am no longer worthy to be called your son." But the father said to his servants, "Bring quickly the best robe, and put it on him, and put a ring on his hand, and shoes on his feet. And bring the fattened calf and kill it, and let us eat and celebrate. **For this my son was dead, and is alive again; he was lost, and is found." And they began to celebrate.** (Luke 15:20–24, emphasis added)

Surprise! The father embraced his son and showed him amazing love.

This is the love you receive from God.
And this is the love you are given to share with others.

God's love was paid for by Jesus on the cross. It fills your heart through God's living Word. It releases you from sadness when it flows through you to others.

Getting Through It

WORD: How does receiving God's love help you show love?

WRESTLE: Let God know how much you appreciate His love. When do you most need to be reminded of His love?

WATCH: Who in your life needs to be shown love? How can you do that this week?

Certain Hope

A key gift for lifting you out of your pit of grief is hope.

Hope isn't a foolish wish or an impossible dream. Hope is knowing that God is faithful, and He will come through for you.

When you put your hope in God, your hope is completely certain. **Hope from God means you have every reason to keep going.** Something very good awaits you—even if you have to wait for it until Jesus comes back.

You may have heard of a man named Job. If there was anyone who understood what it meant to be sad and in pain, it was Job. Job lost everything—his loved ones, his home, his friends, and his dignity. But even in his despair, Job held on to hope in God. Job said, *"Though* [*God*] *slay me, I will hope in Him"* (Job 13:15).

Job's extreme hope shows that God's gift of hope is not a dream. You can look forward, past the darkness and loss, to something better just around the corner.

If God starts something, He never ends it with disappointment.

Listen to this promise from God's Word:

> Therefore, since we have been justified by faith, we have peace with God through our Lord Jesus Christ. Through Him we have also obtained access by faith into this grace in which we stand, **and we rejoice in hope of the glory of God. Not only that, but we rejoice in our sufferings, knowing that suffering produces endurance, and endurance produces character, and character produces hope, and hope does**

> **not put us to shame,** because God's love has been poured into our hearts through the Holy Spirit who has been given to us. (Romans 5:1–5, emphasis added)

God holds on to you in your darkness. His hope will bring you through.

Getting Through It

WORD: How does Jesus' life, death, and resurrection give you hope?

WRESTLE: How might your suffering be producing endurance, character, and hope in you?

WATCH: In prayer, ask God to fill you with His gift of hope.

Hope in the Resurrection

How can you be absolutely certain that you can live with hope, even as you travel through grief and loss? How can you know for sure that you won't be disappointed? The answer is found in Jesus' resurrection.

Think about it:

If Jesus rose from the dead after all He suffered, what *isn't* possible through Him?

Romans 8 says, "*If God is for us, who can be against us? He who did not spare His own Son but gave Him up for us all,* ***how will He not also with Him graciously give us all things?*** *Who shall bring any charge against God's elect? It is God who justifies. Who is to condemn? Christ Jesus is the one who died—****more than that, who was raised—who is at the right hand of God, who indeed is interceding for us***" (vv. 31–34, emphasis added).

Jesus is alive and on your side! God *loves* to give you His best. He wants you to live with hope every day.

With Jesus risen and alive, suffering is not the end of your story.

But did Jesus *really* rise from the dead? Ask the angel, who shared the news. Ask Mary, Peter, and John, who saw the empty tomb (John 20:1–18). Ask the disciples, who saw and touched the risen Savior (John 20:19–29). Ask the five hundred, who saw Jesus, or ask Jesus' brother James, who became a leader in faith because he saw the risen Christ. Ask Paul, who didn't even *want* to meet Jesus or believe His resurrection was true, but became a proclaimer of hope after he met Jesus on the road to Damascus

(1 Corinthians 15:3–8). **The facts tell the story of hope: Jesus really rose from the dead.**

And **that fact tells your broken heart that you can expect good things because Jesus is alive.** He is lifting you out of the pit of grief and promising that new life is ahead.

Getting Through It

WORD: How does Jesus' resurrection change the way you look at your loss?

WRESTLE: Thank God for letting you know that death and pain do not win.

WATCH: Tell someone a reason for hope in your hopelessness.

Jesus, Our Hope

If you're really looking for hope, there is one place to look: Jesus.

How do you do it? The Gospel of John reports seven statements of Jesus that show you why He is the hope you need. Each statement begins with "I am"—words that show He is truly God and is able to restore your life.

1. Jesus said, *"I am the bread of life; whoever comes to Me shall not hunger, and whoever believes in Me shall never thirst"* (John 6:35).

When your regular "diet" includes God's Word and all His gifts, you are being fueled by resources that will not fail.

2. Jesus said, *"I am the light of the world. Whoever follows Me will not walk in darkness, but will have the light of life"* (John 8:12).

**When everything else looks dark,
Jesus will brighten your life.**

3. Jesus said, *"I am the door. If anyone enters by Me, he will be saved"* (John 10:9).

**You are not trapped in your sadness.
Jesus opens the way to new life.**

4. Jesus said, *"I am the good shepherd. . . . I know My own and My own know Me"* (John 10:11, 14).

Jesus *knows* you.

He understands exactly what you need and provides for you on your journey through grief.

5. Jesus said, *"I am the resurrection and the life. Whoever believes in Me, though he die, yet shall he live"* (John 11:25). This promise is huge.

Even though your loss seems permanent, it is only temporary. Jesus will carry you through.

6. Jesus said, "*I am the way, and the truth, and the life. No one comes to the Father except through Me*" (John 14:6).

Jesus will lead you every day.
Follow Him. Trust Him.

7. Jesus said, "*I am the vine; you are the branches. . . . Apart from Me you can do nothing*" (John 15:5). When you find yourself in the pit of heartbreak, **remain in Jesus—not in yourself, in your worries, in your anger, or in your control.**

With Jesus as your hope, you'll get through it.

Getting Through It

WORD: What do these statements of Jesus tell you today?

____

____

____

WRESTLE: Which statement is most challenging? Which is most helpful?

____

____

____

WATCH: Look to Jesus in prayer, asking Him to lead you as you look to the future.

____

____

____

Hope and a Future

When you're struggling, a little bit of hope can carry you forward. That is what God provides for your journey of grief.

Hope doesn't come from inside yourself. It isn't positive thinking. You know how grief feels: when loss and sadness hit hard, they drain you; you become empty; you can't just engage in positive thinking. That's why you need God's precious gift of hope.

Hope is the promise that you will be okay because God comes to you and helps you.

He provides strength. He shows you that a future is still possible.

One of the most encouraging promises in God's Word is Jeremiah 29:11: *"For I know the plans I have for you, declares the Lord, plans for welfare and not for evil, to give you a future and a hope."*

These words were spoken by Jeremiah, a servant of God who had a very hard life. But Jeremiah hung on to God's promises. Even when he was held captive by enemies, he wrote about the hope God provides: *"Remember my affliction and my wanderings, the wormwood and the gall! My soul continually remembers it and is bowed down within me.* ***But this I call to mind, and therefore I have hope: The steadfast love of the Lord never ceases; His mercies never come to an end; they are new every morning; great is Your faithfulness.*** *'The Lord is my portion,' says my soul, 'therefore I will hope in Him.' The Lord is good to those who wait for Him, to the soul who seeks Him.* ***It is good that one should wait quietly for the salvation of the Lord****"* (Lamentations 3:19–26, emphasis added).

**Hang on to hope! Wait for it.
God will come through. He is faithful.
In Him, your hope is sure.**

Getting Through It

WORD: How does Jeremiah 29:11 help you as you go through grief?

WRESTLE: Tell God what makes you hopeless. Ask Him to help you.

WATCH: What glimmers of hope has God placed in your life these days? Write them down here so you remember the gift of hope.

Why Suffering?

Why do you have to go through heartbreak? You've asked that question, haven't you? Why did this happen? Why the hurt? Why has God allowed you to be thrown into the dark pit of loss?

I can relate to the question of why. I'll never forget the terrible day when my favorite cousin and her fiancé were killed. They were shot at close range by a murderer who was never caught. My aunt (my cousin's mom) found them in their apartment. The door was ajar, she walked in, and life became worse than a nightmare—for her and for all of us.

Why. Why the violence, the pain, and the loss? Let's be honest—some challenging questions have to be asked of God: **"Why did You allow this?"** "If this is what You allow, God, why should I believe in You?"

Some people have stopped believing in God because of their hurt. But please listen very carefully to what God does for you in your pit of pain:

God gives you the gift of faith—not to guarantee that heartbreak will never come but to protect your heart and soul from heartbreak's destruction.

Faith in God is not defined by your personal strength, your love for Him because He has been good to you, or even by a promise that bad things won't happen if you believe in God. **God gives you faith so life's pain and chaos will not crush you. Faith is a weapon. Faith is armor.**

God's Word says, *"In all circumstances take up the shield of faith, with which you can extinguish all the flaming darts of the evil one"* (Ephesians 6:16). Faith is your shield. *"Let us be sober, having put on the breastplate of faith and love"* (1 Thessalonians 5:8). Faith is your armor.

A life of faith doesn't mean you won't suffer or struggle. Faith is the gift that makes sure the crushing blows of heartbreak and loss do not win.

Getting Through It

WORD: Why do you need the shield and armor of faith right now?

WRESTLE: How does your grief make you feel toward God?

WATCH: Even when you can't understand why bad things happen, ask God to show you that He can be trusted.

Who Is God?

If God allows suffering and loss, why would you want to have anything to do with Him?

For one important reason:

In this broken world, no one else can carry you through.

It is nice to imagine a god who would stop everything bad in the world. But we don't get to make God into what *we* want Him to be. We don't get to be His boss.

Why not?

I don't know.

All I know is that God *does* reveal Himself in this difficult world. **He chooses to *be with* you, to *walk with* you through the pain, and *promises* that, one day, He will wipe away every tear and will make all things new.**

This true and very real God has shown up in person and has made Himself known. We know Him by His name: Jesus.

Instead of making you comfortable, Jesus joined you in your discomfort.

He died for you and broke the hopelessness of death by rising from the dead. Jesus promised that one day He will return and make everything perfect. For now, He is sitting "at the right hand of the Father"; He is the one who can help you, save you, and bring you through.

God's Word says about Jesus, *"There is salvation in no one else, for there is no other name under heaven given among men by which we must be saved"* (Acts 4:12). **Nothing and no one can do what Jesus does.** That is why He showed up—and still shows up for you every day.

Who is God? He is your Friend and Savior who says, "I am with you always" (Matthew 28:20).

Getting Through It

WORD: The Bible reveals a Savior from grief, chaos, and sin. How does that good news help you today?

WRESTLE: Talk to God about how you *want* life to be. Ask Him to help you if it may not be turning out that way.

WATCH: Look for ways God is helping your heart heal.

How Do You Believe?

Talking about faith when you are struggling with loss can seem out of place. When you're hurting, you don't always *feel* like trusting God. You may feel more like arguing with Him, telling Him to get His act together, or forgetting about Him.

How do you receive God's important help when you don't feel like trusting Him?

First, **remember God's complete love for you.** Ephesians 2:8 says, *"For by grace you have been saved through faith. And this is not your own doing; it is the gift of God."* Your faith is a gift from God.

God helps you—even when you don't feel like trusting Him. That is God's grace.

Next, **remember your Baptism—or talk to a pastor about Baptism if you haven't been baptized.** Colossians 2 says, *"For in [Christ] the whole fullness of deity dwells bodily,* ***and you have been filled in Him,*** *who is the head of all rule and authority. . . .* ***Having been buried with Him in baptism, in which you were also raised with Him through faith in the powerful working of God,*** *who raised Him from the dead"* (vv. 9–10, 12, emphasis added).

When grief makes you feel empty, your Baptism shows you that you've been filled with Jesus' presence and saving work.

Your Baptism is a fact that loss cannot take away.

Finally, **keep reading and hearing God's Word.** The Bible says, *"Faith comes from hearing, and hearing through the word of Christ"* (Romans 10:17).

God's Word puts the fuel of faith into your heart and mind so you can make it through anything life throws at you.

How do you believe? Stay connected to God's active and ongoing reach into your life—even when you don't *feel* strong and even when you wonder if God is at work.

Getting Through It

WORD: How do God's gifts and blessings help you when you feel hurt or weak?

WRESTLE: Ask God to strengthen your trust in Him and to strengthen you as you face each day.

WATCH: Look for a Bible verse that gives you strength. Put it somewhere you can see it every day.

How Do You Live by Faith?

Faith is your shield. Faith is your armor. As the apostle Paul thought about his own grief and pain, he said, *"We walk by faith, not by sight"* (2 Corinthians 5:7).

But how do you do that? What does it look like to live by faith?

God shows the way. Hebrews 11 has been called "the faith hall of fame." But it is not filled with heroes who are famous or perfect. This hall of fame includes real and imperfect people who show you what it means to live by faith. Look at some examples:

Noah (v. 7) built his ark when not a drop of rain had fallen.

Living by faith means trusting God with an unseen future.

Abraham and Sarah (vv. 8–12, 17–19) were ordinary people who, at times, showed great trust in God and, at other times, messed up. How do their lives show faith? Romans 4:20–21 explains, "[*Abraham*] *grew strong in his faith as he gave glory to God, fully convinced that God was able to do what He had promised.*"

Living by faith means you trust that God can accomplish what He promises—even when your life is messy and even when the promise seems impossible.

Moses (vv. 23–29) showed that even an imperfect and frightened person who made a lot of mistakes could become a special servant of God.

Living by faith doesn't mean living a perfect life; it means serving God as someone who is forgiven.

Hebrews 11 shows **God** is at work—in you, for you, and around you. **He is the hero who brings you through every twist and turn. He is the one who assures you that there's more to your story than meets the eye.** He is the one who lifts you out of the pit.

Getting Through It

WORD: Read Hebrews 11 in your Bible. Who in that chapter most inspires you?

WRESTLE: God has helped a lot of people throughout history. Ask God for what you need in your grief today.

WATCH: Who is a "hero" of faith in your life these days? Write that name here:

Thank that person for being in your life.

You Are Not Alone

So far, you've read about five of God's gifts that lift you out of the pit of grief and help you live again. God gives you a sixth gift: community.

Community doesn't mean you have to sign up for a program or join a group. **You are in community *right now.*** Hebrews 12 says: "*Therefore, since we are **surrounded by so great a cloud of witnesses,** let us also lay aside every weight, and sin which clings so closely, and let us run with endurance the race that is set before us, looking to Jesus, the founder and perfecter of our faith*" (vv. 1–2, emphasis added).

You are surrounded by a great cloud of witnesses.

By God's grace and because of His love, you are included in the community of the saints—all of God's rescued people. That means you are not alone in your pain.

First, **you are in God's family.** Jesus is called your brother (Hebrews 2:11). You are a child of God (1 John 3:1). If you don't have a family, take heart! You have one now—by God's grace.

Second, **you are not a weird person who doesn't fit in because of your pain.** The devil wants you to believe that, but the Bible tells the truth: "*Resist [the devil], firm in your faith, knowing that the same kinds of suffering are being experienced **by your brotherhood throughout the world***" (1 Peter 5:9, emphasis added). You have lots of company! People all around you are hurting.

You're not a misfit. The gift of community lets you see that there are many people who need God's help—just like you.

God's gift of community shows you Jesus' love and lets you know that you are not the only one who is suffering. But there is another very important reason for community: **the gift of community invites you to help others, even while you're hurting.**

Getting Through It

WORD: How does Hebrews 12:1–2 encourage you for your journey through grief?

WRESTLE: What causes you to start feeling sorry for yourself? How does the gift of community help you get through that?

WATCH: Pray for someone you know who is also going through struggle. What are some other ways you might help them?

People Need You

The gift of community reveals something important as you travel through grief: **other people need you.**

Hear these wise words: *"Blessed be the God and Father of our Lord Jesus Christ, the Father of mercies and God of all comfort, who comforts us in all our affliction,* ***so that we may be able to comfort those who are in any affliction, with the comfort with which we ourselves are comforted by God***" (2 Corinthians 1:3–4, emphasis added).

God's comfort for you can become the comfort you give to others.

Heartbreak can make you feel useless. **But times of deep struggle can actually help you grow in caring about and understanding others.** Sometimes, going through grief allows you to connect with people who are experiencing similar struggles.

Other people need you—who you are, where you are, and what you're going through. **There is only one you. Do not underestimate your own value.** God called you by name. He sacrificed His Son for you. God treasures you and wants you to bless others. **You have something to give—even from the pit of loss.**

This is how God created us to work: *"For the body does not consist of one member but of many. . . . The eye cannot say to the hand, 'I have no need of you,' nor again the head to the feet, 'I have no need of you.' On the contrary, the parts of the body that seem to be weaker are indispensable. . . . If one member suffers, all suffer together; if one member is honored, all rejoice together"* (1 Corinthians 12:14, 21–22, 26).

God's gift of community shows you that even your grief can be used by Him to help lift other people out of the pit.

The gift of community lets you know that in your darkest moments, you are still God's gift to others.

Getting Through It

WORD: How does 2 Corinthians 1:3–4 apply to your life today?

WRESTLE: Ask God to use your struggle to help and bless others.

WATCH: As you lean on God's comfort and strength, watch to see how God might be directing you to help someone else.

You Need People

You may feel like hiding when you're in the pit of pain, but you need people. It is not good for you to be alone. **You need to let other people in.**

Alone doesn't work—especially when you experience loss. You need someone to listen to you and to be present with you. You need people to pray for you and walk with you through hurt. You need a person to lift you up. That is why God gives you the gift of community. I'm not talking about being a people person or being shy. This is not about going to parties or finding a BFF. This is about receiving God's help through His people.

Jesus said to His disciples, *"This is My commandment, that you love one another as I have loved you"* (John 15:12). Paul urged: *"Be kind to* ***one another****, tenderhearted, forgiving* ***one another****, as God in Christ forgave you"* (Ephesians 4:32, emphasis added). *"Encourage* ***one another*** *and build* ***one another*** *up"* (1 Thessalonians 5:11, emphasis added).

Helping *one another* is important to God.

That is why He created a group of people who serve one another so no one is left empty and alone, where each person has unique gifts and abilities. **This group of people is called the Church. The Church is not a building; it is God's people.** These people reflect God's love and say, "I love you, and I will not leave you. I will listen to you and be here for you. I will care for you. I promise to be with you as you go through this and afterward."

You need people—God's people—in your life.

You will find them as neighbors, classmates, fellow church members, friends, and family. You may be surprised by who reaches out to you, but in your grief, these precious people will bless you and help you out of the pit.

Getting Through It

WORD: How do the "one another" verses help you and guide you?

WRESTLE: If you are feeling alone, thank God for His care and ask Him to show you another person in your life who is a good helper for you.

WATCH: Be on the lookout for someone God puts into your life.

A Word about Church

Let's talk about church.

Not long ago, a friend told me about a time she was going through a lot of stress and anxiety. One day, a friend of hers listened as she talked about her problems. After hearing about her struggle, her friend looked at her and said, "You need to go to church." It stopped my friend in her tracks. She realized that it had been years since she was in church. She had drifted away from being refilled weekly with God's blessings. **She was being emptied out by life, but nothing was filling her up.** That is when she decided to go back. My friend told me that it made a huge difference. Life wasn't perfect, but **now she had a resource for strength and encouragement.**

No church is perfect. But church isn't about being perfect; it is about being a place where imperfect people are lifted out of the pit by God's grace.

You may not always hear the most exciting sermon or sing the songs you like when you go to church. But church was designed by God to be much more than those things. **Going to church gives you a reliable place to receive Jesus' blessings and care.** It is a place where God's Word and Sacraments reach into your life.

Church meets your real needs with God's real help.

The Book of Acts describes the Church: "[*The believers*] *devoted themselves to the apostles' teaching and the fellowship, to the breaking of bread and the prayers. And awe came upon every soul, and many wonders and signs were being done through the apostles. And all who believed were together and had all things in common*" (Acts 2:42–44).

Even if church doesn't feel like your favorite experience, go. Be with God and one another. Watch, listen, and receive. Respond by offering gratitude, prayer, and blessing. See how powerful and restorative God's gift of community can be.

Getting Through It

WORD: What strength did the people in Acts 2 find in community?

WRESTLE: How might going to church help you relieve anxiety and grow in gratitude?

WATCH: As you experience community in church and with God's people, write down one way God is surprising you with His help.

You Have a Purpose

Do you still have a purpose as you go through your grief? It's hard to imagine, isn't it? Your sadness makes you wonder how you will make it to the next day—let alone how you can make a difference in the world.

But take a closer look. **When you're thrown into the pit of pain, God shows you that your purpose is bigger than school, friends, money, stuff, and status.** While the voice of the world may whisper, "You'll never reach your goals" and "With all you've gone through, you probably won't fit in anymore" and "You'll never come back from this," God says, "Everything may change, and all may be lost, but '*I have loved you with an everlasting love; therefore I have continued My faithfulness to you*'" (Jeremiah 31:3).

Your purpose is not found in temporary things; it is founded on God's love and plan for you.

Jesus talked about what God wants for your life. He said, "*And this is the will of Him who sent Me, that I should lose nothing of all that He has given Me, but raise it up on the last day.* ***For this is the will of My Father, that everyone who looks on the Son and believes in Him should have eternal life,*** *and I will raise him up on the last day*" (John 6:39–40, emphasis added). God's will for your life is not that you have the most friends, buy the nicest clothes, or become famous.

God's will is that He never loses you.

God wants to walk with you forever. **That's why He sent Jesus.**

In the pit, God gives you the gift of purpose. He rejoices over you with gladness (Zephaniah 3:17), even when you can't accomplish a thing.

Getting Through It

WORD: What does it mean that God loves you with an "everlasting love"?

WRESTLE: Thank God for the purpose you have—even in your pain and even when you don't know all the details.

WATCH: Put aside your list of things to do today and thank Jesus for loving you just because you're you.

The Purpose You Didn't Ask For

An anxious and stressed Jesus prayed in the Garden of Gethsemane, *"Father, if You are willing, remove this cup from Me. Nevertheless, not My will, but Yours, be done"* (Luke 22:42). Jesus was facing a mission He didn't look forward to. Although He didn't want His bitter cup of suffering, He willingly stepped forward to save us.

There are times when you are called to a mission you would have never asked for and a purpose you do not want. You would never have chosen what you're going through. Jesus understands.

But pain didn't decrease Jesus' purpose; it intensified it. That may be true for you. Because of your grief, you may be growing in love for others. Your heartbreak may increase your desire to help others. Your personal struggle may cause you to bless people in need instead of thinking only of yourself.

Sometimes going through sorrow shows you what is really important.

And when you're given a purpose you didn't ask for, you may be great at it because you won't worship it.

Think about Joseph from the Book of Genesis. He never wanted to be in Egypt. He had no desire to serve in Potiphar's house. He didn't want to become a ruler of the Egyptian nation. But that was God's path for Joseph. And, *"Whatever he did,"* the Bible says, *"the Lord made it succeed"* (Genesis 39:23). Joseph couldn't see it then, but God used him to help save lives (Genesis 45:5) and to preserve the family line, a remnant, that would lead to Jesus (Genesis 45:7). It all started by being thrown into the pit.

You have an important purpose. It may be one you didn't ask for or want, but God will use your life to bless many.

He will use your broken heart to help mend the hearts of others. He will use what you're going through to give other people hope.

Getting Through It

WORD: How might God use your suffering to bring hope to others?

WRESTLE: Ask God to show you His great purpose, even as you journey through grief.

WATCH: How did Jesus respond to His difficult and painful path in life? How does His action help you?

A Purpose You Enjoy

When you are sad, remember that life is not just sadness. God still provides joy. He lets you do what you really love—and you don't have to feel guilty about it.

God's Word says: *"For by grace you have been saved through faith. And this is not your own doing; it is the gift of God, not a result of works, so that no one may boast.* ***For we are His workmanship, created in Christ Jesus for good works, which God prepared beforehand, that we should walk in them***" (Ephesians 2:8–10, emphasis added).

God wants you to do what you are uniquely created to do.

He even equips you with Spirit-created gifts so others can be blessed through you. The Bible says that each person *"is given the manifestation of the Spirit for the common good"* (1 Corinthians 12:7).

God formed you so your gifts can bless others.

What do you like to do? Be with people? Make crafts? Play video games or sports? Go hunting? Do you like to write poetry, play music, work out, or study? How about learning new languages or caring for others? **Jesus lifts you out of your pit of grief so you can do what you enjoy.** God gives you freedom to explore life's adventures.

Go ahead, explore—and see how that blessing blesses others in your life.

When Jesus' disciples were busy and overwhelmed, He said to them, *"Come away by yourselves to a desolate place and rest a while"* (Mark 6:31). They needed a break. **Life wasn't meant to be only hardship and struggle. Jesus called His followers to a quiet place to be restored. He does the same for you.** Take a walk. Watch a movie. Do what you like.

You don't have to give all your attention and time to your pain.

God gives you a greater purpose. It's one you can enjoy.

Getting Through It

WORD: What gifts and interests has God given you?

WRESTLE: Ask God to give you some breaks of joy while you go through sadness.

WATCH: Think about how your gifts and interests can bless others.

Sent

An honest question as you endure loss is "Why am I here?" Wouldn't it be much easier to be fully restored and at peace in heaven? It's a good question. Why doesn't God deliver you from struggle right now? Why do you have to go through sadness?

Jesus' disciples felt the same way when they asked Him, *"Lord, will You at this time restore the kingdom to Israel?"* They wanted everything to be complete, peaceful, and restored. But Jesus said to them, *"It is not for you to know times or seasons that the Father has fixed by His own authority.* ***But you will receive power when the Holy Spirit has come upon you, and you will be My witnesses in Jerusalem and in all Judea and Samaria, and to the end of the earth"*** (Acts 1:6–8, emphasis added). Jesus' disciples were ready for the end, but Jesus was preparing them for a new beginning—one that shared His gifts and shined His light to all people.

That is an important purpose.

Because Jesus wants all people to know Him and receive life through Him, He sends you to share His hope with everyone.

Remember what is important to God: He *"desires all people to be saved and to come to the knowledge of the truth"* (1 Timothy 2:4). That's why **God makes you a part of that rescue mission.** Jesus said, *"You are the light of the world. . . . Let your light shine before others, so that they may see your good works and give glory to your Father who is in heaven"* (Matthew 5:14–16, emphasis added).

You are here to shine your Gospel light to the people *you* meet, *you* know, and *you* love. There's no other *you*.

God lifts you out of the pit of grief so you will share His hope with others.

Getting Through It

WORD: How can you be one of Jesus' witnesses where you live and "to the end of the earth"—even in your sadness?

WRESTLE: Ask God to teach you and lead you so you can shine His light brightly.

WATCH: Look for people you know who need to hear about Jesus. Write down a name or two here:

Pray for them and ask God to help you share the Good News of Jesus with them.

Presence Matters

So far, you've read about seven gifts that lift you out of the pit of loss and carry you through grief. These gifts work because of their source: the presence and power of Jesus. Jesus' presence is the eighth gift, the gift that starts and keeps you going on your journey through grief. God loves you, finds you, walks with you, and gives you a new and bright beginning.

The gifts in this book do not come from within. They aren't from the world—the world brings sadness and heartbreak. These gifts come from God. Why? Because He loves you and refuses to lose you to hopelessness and sadness.

It is true that God is eternal and almighty.
But He also came down to be with you.

God became human to walk in your shoes, to get His hands dirty in your mess, and to carry your suffering. The Bible describes how He did it: *"Christ Jesus, who, though He was in the form of God, did not count equality with God a thing to be grasped, but emptied Himself, by taking the form of a servant, being born in the likeness of men.* ***And being found in human form, He humbled Himself by becoming obedient to the point of death, even death on a cross****"* (Philippians 2:5–8, emphasis added).

Jesus became present to save you. The presence of your Savior pushes the dark clouds away so you can live again.

Because Jesus has *been through* suffering, just like you, He knows exactly what you need. So, little by little, He blesses you and leads you through your journey of grief. He lifts you from the pit and shows you the life that awaits you. All along the way, He promises, *"I am with you always, to the end of the age"* (Matthew 28:20).

Getting Through It

WORD: How does the fact that Jesus gave up everything to be with you make you feel?

WRESTLE: Thank God for walking with you in your sadness and hurt. Ask Him to give you a sense of peace.

WATCH: When do you feel most alone? Talk to someone you trust and ask for that person's help for those times of loneliness.

Real Presence

If God is really present, is there a way to connect with Him?

Human religions and myths teach that God is far away and out of reach. But the true God surprised the world by becoming human—coming down—to be with us.

Jesus connected with people. He spoke and listened. He brought help and blessing. He showed the world something new—that the *real* God is really, physically present.

The Bible tells about God's actions: He walked in the Garden of Eden and talked with Adam and Eve (Genesis 3:8–9). He appeared to Abram (Genesis 12:7). He called to Moses from a burning bush and said, *"I have surely seen the affliction of My people who are in Egypt and have heard their cry because of their taskmasters. I know their sufferings, and* ***I have come down*** *to deliver them out of the hand of the Egyptians"* (Exodus 3:7–8, emphasis added). Throughout history, God shows that He is present and that He personally connects with His people.

The apostle John put it this way: *"The Word became flesh and* ***dwelt among us****, and we have seen His glory, glory as of the only Son from the Father, full of grace and truth"* (John 1:14, emphasis added).

Jesus is God coming down, drawing near, and being present.

Today, you can connect with God's presence through the Holy Spirit's work. God speaks through His living Word, the Bible. He enters your life and brings His gift of forgiveness through Baptism (Acts 2:38). He is present in the Lord's Supper. Jesus said, *"Take, eat; this is My body. . . . Drink of it, all of you, for this is My blood of the covenant, which is poured out for many for the forgiveness of sins"* (Matthew 26:26–28). You can talk to Him in prayer.

God's presence is real. He is available.

This is the presence you need as you journey through grief.

Getting Through It

WORD: How does knowing that God is with you give you confidence and strength?

WRESTLE: Thank God for giving you real places to receive His blessings and help.

WATCH: How have you seen God "coming down" to meet you through His Word as you've read this book?

Personal Presence

Do you ever feel like your sadness will never stop hurting? **One of the most difficult parts of grief is that it seems like it will never end. But God doesn't let the darkness win.**

I can tell you personally that God has been faithful in bringing me through my hurt. I am a walking miracle. Jesus brought me through the worst, and **He will bring you through too.**

I have seen people who have gone through terrible loss but are now living as thankful, active, and joyful human beings. This didn't happen because they were strong. It happened because God blessed them with the gifts you've been reading about and lifted them out of the pit. He walked with them step-by-step and surprised them with new life. I've seen it, and I've been amazed every time.

The pit of pain doesn't stand a chance when God is present.

You may have a hard time believing that right now, but let God do His work. Receive His gifts. Give Him some time.

When God gets His saving hands on loss, He always turns it inside out and leads His precious people into new life.

Please know that, because God loves you, He has your grief in His grip too. He is carrying its pain. He is with you in the darkness. Today, your present God promises: *"Fear not, for I am with you; be not dismayed, for I am your God; I will strengthen you, I will help you, I will uphold you with My righteous right hand"* (Isaiah 41:10).

Getting Through It

WORD: The verse from Isaiah 41 gives powerful promises. Which ones mean the most to you? Why?

WRESTLE: Ask God to carry you through the times when your sadness seems like it will never end.

WATCH: Look for God's encouragement in His Word or in someone He puts in your life today. Who do you need to be present for as God's helper for others?

Getting Through It

You've now come to the end of this little book. I pray the journey has been helpful, encouraging, and uplifting. Now, what parting words do I have for you?

First, **I'm so sorry.** I'm sorry you have to endure the sad, hurt-filled, confusing, frustrating, depressing, and heavy burden of loss. Words cannot describe the groans caused by grief. I am truly sorry.

Second, your grief may make you feel like you have no hope and that you will never feel good again. Your hurt may even try to convince you that you should run away from God, that you can never trust anyone, and that you have no future.

But no matter how loud these voices shout—even in your own head—don't listen to them.

Respond to them by repeating God's promises. Answer these negative voices with your faith and hope in Jesus.

That leads to the third parting message: **You have a champion on this journey.** You have a lamp for your feet and a light for your path (Psalm 119:105).

Your Savior is carrying you forward, even when it doesn't feel like it.

Cast your cares upon Jesus. Ask Him to bring you through the pain and lift you out of the pit. Put your hope in His cross and resurrection. Use the gifts He gladly and generously gives.

You get good at what you practice. Practice using His gracious gifts as you travel through grief.

My favorite Bible verse for heartbreak is Psalm 34:18: *"The Lord is near to the brokenhearted and saves the crushed in spirit."* Jesus is close to you and will save you. Watch for Him. Yes, you'll still have grief, questions, and pain. **But God's gifts will lift you out of your pit of grief and loss and give you a new life.**

Your faithful and caring Savior will get you through it.

Getting Through It

WORD: How have you received God's comfort and help as you read this book?

WRESTLE: Ask God to keep His gifts present and active in your life so you can be freed from the hurt and pain of grief.

WATCH: Be on the lookout for someone who may need this book. Share with them the hope you've been given.